"Something's Wrong!"

The roller coaster chugged slowly up the hill. Flossie looked down at the ground below.

"Here we go!" yelled Freddie.

Flossie closed her eyes and felt the roller coaster start down the hill and pick up speed. It rounded a sharp curve.

Suddenly a jolt rocked the car.

"Something's wrong!" Freddie shouted.

Flossie peered over her shoulder at the cable between their car and Nan and Bert's.

Twang! The cable snapped apart!

"HELLLLLLPPPP!" screamed Flossie.

THE NEW
Bobbsey
Twins™

#1

THE SECRET OF JUNGLE PARK

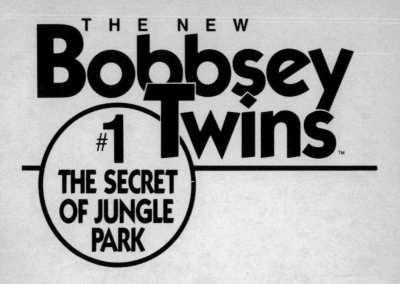

LAURA LEE HOPE
ILLUSTRATED BY GEORGE TSUI

A MINSTREL™ BOOK

PUBLISHED BY
POCKET BOOKS

A MINSTREL PAPERBACK *ORIGINAL*

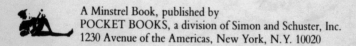

A Minstrel Book, published by
POCKET BOOKS, a division of Simon and Schuster, Inc.
1230 Avenue of the Americas, New York, N.Y. 10020

ISBN: 0-671-62651-5

First Minstrel Books printing August, 1987

10 9 8 7 6 5 4 3 2 1

Contents

1
Don't Panic!

"Yuck!" said Nan Bobbsey. "I don't look like an alien. I look like a monster." Twelve-year-old Nan peered into the mirror. A creature with silver hair and purple lips frowned back at her.

"Flossie, what am I going to do?" Nan looked around. "Flossie?"

"Huh?" Nan's younger sister turned away from another mirror in the dressing room. She was brushing purple powder on her cheeks.

Nan tugged at her silver miniskirt. "This isn't working at all. The name of our band is the Aliens, but I just look weird."

"Know what you need?" said Flossie. "More makeup." She smeared a glob of silver eye shadow across Nan's face. "Close your eyes."

"What are you doing?" asked Nan.

"You'll see." Flossie smeared on some more. "Do you want to look like a rock star or not?"

"But—"

"Got any glitter?" Flossie interrupted. "Judges love glitter."

Nan sat still. Flossie can't make me look any worse than I already do, she thought. I hope.

"Okay," Flossie said finally.

Nan opened her eyes and screamed.

"What's the matter?" asked Flossie.

"It's gross!" Nan's whole face was silver, except for purple cheeks and lips. Glitter sparkled in her hair and eyebrows.

"It is *not*," said Flossie. "You look like the princess in *Bride of the Space Monster*."

Nan turned away from the mirror and reached out as if to strangle Flossie. Flossie ducked. "Let's clean up our stuff," Nan said. "Ready or not, we've got to go."

Flossie grinned. She scooped the makeup into a bag. "I wish you and Bert would let me be in the Aliens," she said. Bert was Nan's twin brother.

"When I'm twelve," Flossie went on, "I'm going to start my own band. Just girls. We'll be called the Passion Flowers."

Nan laughed. "The Passion Flowers? Give me a break, Flossie." She checked her watch. "Come on. The Battle of the Bands starts in twenty minutes."

The Aliens were playing against a dozen other groups at Jungle Park, the large amusement park outside Lakeport. First prize was a brand-new set of microphones, something the Aliens could really use.

They had a great group. Bert played drums, and his friends Jimmy Pendleton and Brian Fisher played guitars. Nan was on keyboards.

"Which way to the outdoor stage?" Nan asked. She and Flossie stepped into the hall.

"I forget," Flossie said.

"This place is huge." Nan looked down the hallway. "Maybe that man knows."

At the end of the hall stood a tall man. His back was to the girls.

"Excuse me," said Nan, when she and Flossie reached him. "How do we get to the stage?"

The man turned around. He looked mean. It wasn't just his wild red hair or his bushy red mustache. It was the black eyepatch—and the hard look on his face. Nan was sorry she'd asked him.

The man grunted. He pointed down the hall with his left hand, then hurried off.

"Let's get out of here," Flossie whispered as they walked away. "That man gave me the creeps." She pulled Nan along.

The hallway turned left and ended at a big door that said Stage. Nan pushed it open.

"Look," said Flossie. "There's our equipment. Hey, Bert! Freddie! Where are you?" she called.

"Ohhhhh, help me," someone groaned from behind the drum set.

The girls rushed over to the drums.

Behind them lay Freddie, Flossie's twin brother. His arm was covered with blood.

"Freddie!" screamed Flossie.

The stage curtains flew open. A creature with blue hair, green skin, and pointed ears jumped out at them. "Aha! My next victims!" he growled.

Flossie ducked behind Nan. "Help!" she yelled.

Freddie sat up. "Surprise!" he shouted, grinning. "It's fake blood. Isn't it neat?"

Flossie peeked around Nan. She was still shaking.

"Flossie, it's me," said the blue-haired monster.

"Bert?" asked Flossie. The color returned to her face. Bert started to laugh.

"You and your stupid jokes," said Nan. "You practically gave Flossie a heart attack."

"What did you do to your face?" Bert asked, staring at his twin.

Nan's eyes narrowed. "For your information, this is exactly how a real rock star looks." She

wrinkled her nose. "Where'd you get that disgusting blood, anyway?" she asked Freddie.

"Bert made it," replied her brother. "It's part of his costume." He stared at Flossie. "What happened to *your* face?"

Flossie's hand went to the purple powder she'd brushed on. "Nothing," she said. "Is that ketchup on your arm?"

Bert pulled a plastic bottle from his pocket. "It's corn syrup with red food coloring," he said. "I read about it in Rex Sleuther's last book. Want some on your shoulder? It will *ooze* down—"

Nan shrank back. "Aliens don't bleed."

"Sure they do," said Bert, opening the bottle.

"Die, alien scum!" Suddenly, a short pirate wearing a black eyepatch charged at them.

"It's Danny!" said Freddie. Danny Rugg was the school bully. Hardly anyone liked him, including the Bobbseys.

Danny swung a sword in front of him as he ran. "On guard!" he yelled.

"We're not impressed," said Nan.

Danny stopped. "You will be when the Skulls win the Battle of the Bands," he said.

"Don't count on it," snapped Bert.

Danny stabbed at the air. "The Aliens don't stand a chance," he said. "Everybody knows that."

"That's not true!" cried Flossie. "The audience will love them. They're better than a bunch of dumb pirates."

Nan didn't say anything. She knew the Skulls would be tough to beat.

"Just hope there's an audience left by the time your turn comes," Danny said.

"What's that supposed to mean?" asked Bert.

"You'll see." Danny poked Bert with his sword. He snapped his eyepatch. "And Nan is right. Aliens don't bleed."

Bert clenched his fist. "Want to find out if pirates do?" he asked.

Danny hurried off.

"What a pest," said Nan.

Freddie looked at Bert. "The Aliens are going to win, aren't they?"

"No question," said Bert.

A voice on the loudspeaker announced five minutes to curtain. Bert turned to Nan. "We're on last," he told her.

Nan groaned. "Just our luck. Where are Brian and Jimmy?"

"They're watching the other bands from the audience," Bert replied. "Our equipment is all set up and ready to go."

"Let's sit with them," said Nan. "I'll just be nervous hanging around back here."

The four Bobbseys left the stage and walked into the outdoor theater.

"There sure are a lot of people here," said Flossie as they headed up the aisle toward the back. She started to sing the words to the Aliens' opening number. "We just rocked in from outer space . . ."

"They should put you in the band," said Freddie. "You sound like a real alien."

Flossie made a face. "At least I don't act like one!"

"There's Brian and Jimmy." Nan had no trouble spotting two boys with blue hair. But there were no seats near them. The Bobbseys wound up in the last row.

Up onstage, a man announced the first band—the Mummies. Three boys wrapped in bandages began to play an eerie song.

Flossie put her hands over her ears. "They're awful," she said to Nan.

"Even worse than you," Freddie said.

Flossie poked him in the ribs.

When the Mummies were done, Danny Rugg and the Skulls came onstage. Bert edged forward in his seat as they began to play. "Danny's pretty good on that guitar," he whispered to Nan. The Skulls swung into action. The audience roared.

"Everyone loves them," Nan said. "What are we going to do?"

"Play better," Bert answered.

When the Skulls finished, the audience went wild. The people sitting in front of the Bobbseys got up to leave. "They're the winners," said one man. He took his daughter by the hand. "Might as well try the rides now."

Bert and Nan watched them go. "Maybe that's what Danny meant about no one being around by the time we play," Bert said. More and more bands came on. More and more people left the audience. A group called the Hot Tamales began playing. When would the Aliens' turn come?

Nan leaned back and closed her eyes. She could feel her makeup melting in the sun. Then she heard a murmur sweep through the audience. She sat up and opened her eyes. A funnel of black smoke was pouring from one corner of the stage. What a weird effect, thought Nan. Even for a group called the Hot Tamales.

The smoke became thicker. It billowed off the stage. Something was wrong!

"Help!" yelled one of the Hot Tamales. "Fire!"

The smoke poured into the audience. People started to run in every direction. Nan grabbed Freddie and Flossie. "Don't panic," she said. "We're safe back here." She looked around. "Where's Bert?"

Freddie pointed at the stage.

"Bert!" screamed Nan. "Where are you going?"

"Our equipment!" shouted Bert. "I've got to save it!" Nan watched him climb onto the stage and throw back the curtain. Then he disappeared in the smoke!

2
Looking for Clues

"Bert! Come back!" Freddie shouted. The stage was filled with smoke. In the audience, people scrambled to get away. Freddie's heart raced. Was Bert all right?

Finally, he heard sirens. A police car pulled up. Then came the fire engine. Fire fighters rushed to the stage with a hose.

"Look! There he is!" Flossie pointed. Out of the smoke came Bert. He coughed as he shoved the Aliens' instruments to safety.

The fire fighters with the hose ran past Bert. "Over here!" one shouted. "The smoke is coming from just one place."

Water shot from the hose. Something sizzled on the stage, then everything became still. All that was left was a black cloud of smoke and a strong smell.

Nan, Flossie, and Freddie rushed to the stage as Bert jumped down. "Close call," said Bert, grinning. "We almost lost the equipment."

"Equipment!" Nan cried. "We almost lost *you!*"

"I don't think so." Bert lowered his voice. "I don't even think there was a fire."

"What?" Freddie cried.

"Maybe you're right, Bert Bobbsey," a familiar voice cut in. "But you took a very foolish risk just now."

"Lieutenant Pike!" said Nan. The police officer was an old friend of the Bobbseys.

The lieutenant smiled. "I should have known you Bobbseys would be around. But in disguise?" He stared at Nan's silver hair.

Nan brushed it out of her eyes. "But there had to be a fire," she said. "We all saw the smoke."

"It came from only one place. And there was too much of it. That means a smoke bomb," replied the lieutenant.

Bert glanced at the stage.

"Don't even *think* about going back up there," Lieutenant Pike said to him. "This is a serious crime. No aliens allowed."

"What's so serious about a smoke bomb?" asked Freddie.

"It's serious when it frightens a big crowd. Someone might have gotten hurt. Or worse." Lieutenant Pike frowned. "This isn't the first time we've been called out here. It's the fourth accident in three weeks. If this keeps up, we'll have to close down the park."

"Close down Jungle Park?" said Nan. "But there's no other place like it near Lakeport."

"That's right," said Freddie. "The animals . . ."

"And the rides," said Bert.

"And the great food," added Flossie.

"Those are all nice things," Lieutenant Pike agreed. "But they don't matter if the park isn't safe."

"Wait a second," said Bert. "It's not fair to blame the park. Someone *set* the smoke bomb. Maybe we can find out who's causing the accidents." He glanced at the stage again. "After you're finished, could we look around for clues?" he asked.

Lieutenant Pike shrugged. "I suppose that's okay," he replied.

"Come on," said Bert. He led the others away from the stage, and they sat down to wait.

It seemed to Freddie that they waited forever. Finally, the police left.

"Now," said Bert. Freddie was the first to hop up onto the stage.

"See this?" Bert pointed to a black circle on

the floor. "That's where the smoke bomb was. My drum set was right in front of it."

"I don't see any bomb," said Flossie.

"The police took away the evidence," Freddie said. "Don't you know anything?"

Bert started searching the floor. "Sometimes the police don't find everything," he said. He stood up and held out his hand. "Like this."

"A black eyepatch!" cried Freddie.

Bert nodded. "This wouldn't mean anything to the police, but it does to me. Remember what Danny said about no one being around for our turn?"

"Are you saying Danny set the bomb?" Nan asked. "He's mean, but I don't think he'd do that. Somebody could've been killed!"

"Maybe all he thought about was knocking us out of the contest. Danny's not too smart, sometimes. Besides," Bert went on, "who else was back here with an eyepatch?"

"We saw a man wearing a patch. He was outside our dressing room," said Nan.

"Yeah," Flossie added. "He looked weird, too. I bet he did it."

Bert shook his head. "No way. It's Danny. He had an eyepatch. And a *reason* to set that bomb."

While everyone was talking, Freddie stared at the floor. Why did Bert and Nan always find the good clues? He kicked aside a board. Underneath was a thin plastic stick. "Hey!" he shouted. "A clue!"

Bert picked up the stick. "The Sunset Grill," he read. He handed it to Freddie and smiled. "It's a swizzle stick. This is for stirring drinks, not setting smoke bombs."

Freddie bit his lip. His big chance was slipping away. He had found a clue—and no one believed him.

Just then, the contest director walked onto the stage. "Aren't you kids part of the Aliens?" he asked.

Bert and Nan nodded.

"Hurry up, then," he said. "We're going to finish the contest, and you're next."

Freddie put the swizzle stick in his pants pocket. "You'll see," he said. He didn't care what Bert thought. He *knew* he had a clue, and he was going to prove it, too!

In spite of all the excitement, the Aliens played very well. When the contest ended, they were tied with the Skulls. Both bands would play again on the weekend.

"I hope we can beat them," Nan said that evening at dinner. "Danny is really good."

"But you're better," said Mr. Bobbsey. He reached for a piece of fried chicken.

"I'm just glad you're all safe," Mrs. Bobbsey

said. "I heard about the trouble while I was at the office. I was so worried." Mrs. Bobbsey worked part-time as a reporter for the *Lakeport News*.

"The first report talked about a fire," she continued. "Now the police think the smoke bomb was some sort of joke."

Freddie saw Bert nudge Nan. "Do they have any suspects?" Bert asked.

Mrs. Bobbsey shook her head. "None," she replied. "None at all."

Freddie reached into his pocket for the swizzle stick. If only he could get to the Sunset Grill, he was sure he'd find another clue. Then everyone would believe him. Maybe if he talked to Bert . . .

As soon as dinner was over, Freddie rushed up to Bert's room. Bert was putting on his jacket. "Where are you going?" Freddie asked.

"The Skulls are playing at the youth center tonight," said Bert. "I want to see if Danny still has his eyepatch."

"Oh," said Freddie. He flopped down on the bed. "I was sort of hoping you'd take me to the Sunset Grill," he said.

Bert sighed. "If you want to come with me to the youth center, fine. But I'm not taking you to the Sunset Grill. It's clear on the other side of town."

Freddie rolled over and stared at the ceiling. "Never mind," he said. What he thought was, Now I'll never get my chance.

At breakfast the next morning, Freddie asked, "Was Danny wearing an eyepatch, Bert?"

"Yup. But I bet he's got a bunch of them," Bert said. "I still think he's guilty. All I need is proof."

Mrs. Bobbsey sat down at the breakfast table. "How about eating out tonight?" she said. "Dad and I thought it would be fun." She turned to Freddie. "It's your turn to pick the restaurant."

Freddie couldn't believe his good luck. "The Sunset Grill," he said immediately.

Bert groaned.

"Where's that?" asked Mrs. Bobbsey.

Mr. Bobbsey glanced over at Freddie. "The Sunset Grill down on Ely Avenue?" he asked. "Are you sure?"

Freddie folded his arms. "Positive."

Mrs. Bobbsey smiled. "It's Freddie's choice," she said.

"I don't care," said Flossie, "as long as they have good desserts."

"Thanks, Mom," said Freddie. He fingered the swizzle stick in his pocket. "Now we'll find out who the *real* detective is!" he whispered to Bert.

That evening, the Bobbsey family went to the Sunset Grill. They sat at a big, round table right by the window. No one else was in the dining room. The Bobbseys soon found out why.

"Do I have to eat any more of this meat loaf?" asked Flossie. "It tastes funny."

Mrs. Bobbsey picked unhappily at a piece of gray roast beef. "Just eat what you can, sweetie," she said.

Freddie stared at his plate of watery spaghetti. "May I be excused?" he asked.

"Why? Are you going to throw up?" asked Bert.

Freddie turned his back on Bert. He headed toward the rear of the restaurant. Now was his chance to look around. He passed a closed door that said Main Office. Inside he could hear a man talking. "The problem is *tiny!*" the man shouted in a deep, gravelly voice.

Freddie stopped and scratched his head. If the problem was tiny, why was the man so excited? Freddie glanced up the hall but didn't see anything strange. Maybe Bert was right. Maybe the swizzle stick wasn't a clue after all.

Freddie jumped as a hand slapped his shoul-

der. He whirled around. Nan was grinning at him.

"Find anything?" she asked.

Freddie scowled. "Everyone thinks this is a big joke."

"Not really," Nan said. "I came back to help you look around." She grinned again. Anything to get away from that food."

"I looked around," Freddie told her. "There's nothing here."

The man in the office started shouting again. Nan turned. "Come on," she said. "Let's check this out." She opened the office door a crack.

Freddie squeezed past Nan. "Let me see," he said, bumping into the door.

It opened wide, to show a tall, bald man sitting behind a desk. He hung up the telephone, stood up, and took a step toward the door.

"What are you kids doing here?" he growled.

3

Heading for Trouble

Nan spoke quickly. "Sorry. My brother thought this was the rest room."

"It's downstairs." The man grabbed the phone with his left hand and turned his back.

Nan closed the door. "Let's get out of here," she said.

They went back to their table. Mr. and Mrs. Bobbsey were at the register, paying the bill. "Mom wants to go somewhere else for dessert," Flossie said.

"I can't argue with that," Nan said. She told Flossie and Bert about the bald man.

"You sound just like Flossie." Bert made his voice go high. "That man looks mean, so he must be a bad guy." He frowned. "It doesn't make him a suspect."

"That guy with the eyepatch *was* creepy," Flossie insisted. "He had a bushy mustache, and his hair was all wild."

"We should check up on him," Nan added.

Bert stood up. "Count me out," he said. "I already have my suspect."

Nan didn't say anything, but she was sure Bert was wrong.

Early the next morning, Nan heard footsteps outside her bedroom. She opened her door as Bert crept past. "Where are you going?"

"I'll be back for lunch." Bert tiptoed down the stairs. Then Nan heard the front door shut.

Nan sighed and sat on her bed. Bert could be so stubborn.

She got up and slipped into Flossie's room. "Flossie, wake up. I need you and Freddie to help me do some investigating."

Flossie opened one eye. "It's too early," she mumbled.

Nan shook Flossie's shoulder. "If you get dressed right now, I'll buy you a milk shake later."

Flossie sat up. "Coming," she said.

Freddie was already up, eating breakfast. Nan and Flossie had just started theirs when a report came over the radio.

"Police are still investigating the strange accidents at Jungle Park," said the news reporter.

Nan and Freddie looked up. "WROK spoke with Simon P. Harris, one of the owners of the park," the reporter went on.

"Mr. Harris, you're a busy man. You own several restaurants around Lakeport. And, of course, you own Jungle Park. Do you have any idea why someone might be causing trouble?"

A deep, gravelly voice said, "I'm only a part owner. I work with Mr. Loomis. And I have no idea why anyone would be fooling around in the park. It's a terrible thing. People are saying Jungle Park is dangerous."

Freddie nearly choked on his cereal. "That's the voice I heard at the Sunset Grill," he said. "I'd know it anywhere!"

He turned up the volume. But the next voice to come on gave the weather report.

"Freddie! Are you sure?" said Flossie.

"Positive," said Freddie.

"I heard it, too," said Nan. "He's right." She thought for a second. "Maybe Simon P. Harris owns Jungle Park *and* the Sunset Grill. Let's go to the park and see what we can find out."

The three Bobbseys got on their bikes. Soon they were pedaling up to the Jungle Park gate.

"Look who's here," said Freddie.

Lieutenant Pike stood by his car, waving.

"Are you still investigating?" called Freddie.

Before he could answer, Flossie asked, "May

we follow you around? We promise not to say anything."

"I don't think so." Lieutenant Pike smiled.

"Please, oh, please," said Flossie. "We'll be really quiet."

Lieutenant Pike shook his head. "Sorry, kids." He started to walk away.

Nan thought fast. "You know, *we* were at the stage. We saw the smoke and everything. And nobody ever questioned *us*."

Lieutenant Pike stopped. "Did you notice anything unusual?" he asked.

"Yes," said Nan. "We ran into this weird guy in the hall. He wore an eyepatch."

"Then later, we found an eyepatch near where the smoke bomb went off," added Flossie.

Lieutenant Pike took out his notepad. He flipped through the pages.

"An eyepatch, you say?" He looked up. "I'd like to hear some more about this."

Freddie shot a glance at Nan. "Our mom expects us home in forty-five minutes."

Nan caught on right away. "Sooner," she said. "We're going to our grandmother's."

Lieutenant Pike looked at his watch. "I'm supposed to meet someone right now. But it shouldn't take that long. Why don't you come along and we can talk afterward?"

Freddie nodded slowly. "I guess that would be okay," he said.

Lieutenant Pike smiled. "Good. Now do me a favor. Not one word while I'm in my meeting, all right?"

"We promise," said Nan. She secretly gave Freddie a thumbs-up sign.

Lieutenant Pike led them through the crowds, past a man in a lion suit. "This is a crazy place," said the lieutenant.

"It's great," said Freddie. "I like the man in the lion suit. He's funny."

They walked way over to one side of the park. Behind a fence stood a trailer with a sign on it that said Office. Lieutenant Pike knocked on the door.

"Come in," a voice replied. Inside, a stout man was smoking a cigar. "Hello, Lieutenant," he said. "These your kids?"

Lieutenant Pike cleared his throat. "Friends of the family." He turned to the Bobbseys. "This is Mr. Loomis. He owns Jungle Park."

"Well, half of it," said Mr. Loomis. "My partner is around somewhere." He stubbed out his cigar. "So what are you doing to stop these accidents? You've been investigating for weeks, and now some yo-yo comes along and causes more trouble. It's like someone wants to close down the park."

"You can't close down, Mr. Loomis!" cried Flossie, forgetting her promise. "You make the best cotton candy in Lakeport."

Mr. Loomis smiled. "Thanks for saying so, kid." He motioned to some old chairs piled high with newspapers. "Clear yourselves some seats."

Lieutenant Pike took out his notepad. "Just a few routine questions," he said. "I know you answered them for the fire department, but I have to ask them again. Where were you when the smoke bomb went off?"

"Right here at my desk," said Mr. Loomis.

Lieutenant Pike wrote in his notepad. "Do you have any idea why anyone would pull that trick? Why someone would want to scare everyone at the theater?" he asked next.

Mr. Loomis shook his head. "It's stupid. And it's really hurting us."

"What do you mean?" asked Lieutenant Pike.

"People are starting to be afraid to come here. Business is way down. And it takes money to keep a park going."

He shook his head. "We do what we can, though. I've been running some of the rides myself. And my partner, Simon Harris, has been helping, too. He hired a guy to make repairs on the rides. And he's paying him out of his own pocket."

"Hmmmm," said Lieutenant Pike, making another note. "What's the repairman's name?"

"I don't know." Mr. Loomis shrugged. "He's a quiet guy. I don't think I've ever heard him talk, but he works hard."

"I'd like to speak to him," said Lieutenant Pike.

"Well, he's around the park somewhere, working. You can't miss him. Just look for a redheaded guy with an eyepatch."

Nan and Flossie glanced at each other.

"I'll find him," Lieutenant Pike said. "But I want to talk to Beverly Baku next. Any idea where I can find her?"

"I expect she's over at the cages," Mr. Loomis replied. "It's feeding time."

As the Bobbseys followed Lieutenant Pike across the park, Nan filled him in on what they'd discovered so far.

"Thanks for telling me what you know," Lieutenant Pike said to the Bobbseys. "Don't you have to go soon?"

"We have a few more minutes." Nan followed the lieutenant to the animal cages.

Beverly Baku was tossing hay to the elephants. She was a tall, slender black woman. Her hoop earrings swung back and forth.

"I told everything to the fire department," she said impatiently. "I'm in charge of the ani-

mals. I wasn't even near the stage when that smoke bomb went off."

"We're talking to every employee again for the police investigation. Maybe you'll remember something," said Lieutenant Pike.

Beverly grunted and tossed in some more hay.

"Mr. Loomis tells me business is bad," said the lieutenant.

"That's right," she replied. "And the animals are paying for it. My lions need red meat every day. Instead, they're only getting it twice a week."

An elephant stamped its foot and raised its trunk. "Sheba's unhappy, too," Beverly added. "The elephants were supposed to get new cages. Now they won't." She glared at Lieutenant Pike. "Do you know what happens when elephants are in too small a space?"

Lieutenant Pike shook his head.

"Trouble," said Beverly. She brushed hay from her hands. "Any more questions?"

"Not for now," said the lieutenant. He put away his notepad and looked annoyed.

"Time to get out of here," Nan whispered. She waved to Lieutenant Pike. "We have to go." She, Flossie, and Freddie ran off.

"Let's get that milk shake now," said Nan.

"All right!" said Flossie.

They walked to the refreshment patio near

the Jungle Safari rides. Soon, Nan had a tray full of milk shakes. The younger twins found an empty table, and they sat down.

"I think we should investigate Beverly Baku," said Flossie. "I didn't like her." She took a big gulp of her milk shake.

"That doesn't mean she's guilty," Freddie pointed out.

"I know that," Flossie said. She gave Freddie a dirty look.

Freddie played with his spoon for a moment. The check for the drinks lay on the tray. Freddie picked it up. "They made a mistake," he said suddenly.

"Where?" asked Nan.

"Here. See? They added wrong. We owe another dollar." Freddie opened Nan's purse.

"Hey," said Nan. "What do you think you're doing? That's private property."

Freddie sighed. "I'm paying what we owe. Okay?" He took a dollar out of Nan's wallet and headed toward the cash register.

Flossie turned back to Nan. "Did you read the new *Teen Fashion?*" she asked.

"No," said Nan.

"They had a picture of this little red purse. Just like one Emily Davis has . . ."

Nan only half-listened as she stirred her milk shake with her straw. Who was this mysterious

Mr. Eyepatch? Lieutenant Pike was interested in him. But he hadn't said anything when they'd told him what they knew. She glanced over at the cash register. Freddie should have been back by now.

"When I save enough, I'm going to buy a purple purse," Flossie said.

Her voice was drowned out by a sound like a gunshot. Flossie jumped. "What was that?"

"Probably that truck starting up," said Nan, pointing. A red van was edging its way through the crowds of people. It pulled out of the parking lot, then rolled past the refreshment patio.

"Hey!" said Flossie. "There's Freddie."

Nan turned around. "Where?"

"There." Flossie pointed.

"Oh, no!" Nan jumped up from her seat. She saw Freddie, all right—hanging onto the back of the red van!

4

Mr. Eyepatch Disappears

The van turned a corner and disappeared. Nan grabbed Flossie's arm. "C'mon, Flossie. Move! We've got to catch up with him."

Nan started to run. She headed for Jungle Kingdom, where the wild animals were kept.

Flossie followed Nan past the camel rides and the elephants' cages. "Nan, stop," Flossie called. "I can't keep up!"

"We can't stop," said Nan. "Freddie needs us." The two girls ran around a corner. Nan skidded to a stop in front of the lions' den. "Look," she said.

It was the red van.

"I don't see anyone." Flossie was upset. "What if Freddie fell off? He's always falling off things."

A crumpled paper cup hit her on the head. "Ow!" she cried.

"I heard that," said Freddie. He crawled out from behind a trash barrel.

"Freddie! Are you okay?" asked Flossie.

"Of course. I know what I'm doing."

"Then tell us," said Nan.

"I was in line to give the cashier the dollar. The man in front of me asked for some change. And guess what?"

"What?" said Nan.

"He was tall and bald and had a gravelly voice, but I couldn't see his face. Then he got in that van."

"And you followed him!" Nan exclaimed. "That was a dangerous stunt you pulled."

Freddie shook his head. "He was driving through the crowd. He'd have to go slow."

"You weren't scared?" Flossie asked.

"Going five miles an hour? No way!" said Freddie. He pointed to the lions' den. "The man went over there."

A door next to the lions' den opened. A man stepped out.

Nan grabbed Freddie's arm. "That's not the man we saw at the Sunset Grill. It's the creepy guy with the eyepatch!"

Mr. Eyepatch walked off down the brick path leading to the rides.

"Let's move it," said Freddie.

"Not too close," Nan whispered. "We don't want him to know we're following him."

The three Bobbseys slowly rounded a bend in the path. Ahead, people were laughing at a man dancing in a gorilla suit. Mr. Eyepatch cut through the crowd. Before the Bobbseys could follow, a group of Boy Scouts blocked them.

"Which way did he go?" Nan asked. "To the bumper cars or into the fun house?"

"Rats," said Freddie. "We lost him."

They tried both the bumper cars and the fun house. But they didn't find Mr. Eyepatch.

"Look!" Freddie pointed to a tall, bald man in the crowd. "It's the man from the Sunset Grill. I *did* see him in line."

The man darted among the people, then stopped. He seemed to be looking for someone.

"I'd love to find out if he's Simon Harris," said Nan. "But one of us would have to get close to him. Someone he hasn't seen before." Nan and Freddie stared at Flossie.

Her eyes grew round. "Don't look at me," she said.

"Please?" said Nan. "It's really important."

Flossie shook her head. "No way. I'm not going after him."

"C'mon, Flossie," said Freddie. "Don't you want to solve the case?"

"What if he starts to chase me? And then he

gets me and throws me to the ground. You know what happens next? He strangles me to death!"

"Would you relax?" said Nan. "First of all, Freddie and I are going to be right here watching you. Besides, I've got a plan."

Nan whispered in Flossie's ear. Taking some paper from her purse, she scribbled something. "Here," she said, handing Flossie the paper and pencil. "Good luck."

Flossie walked over to the man, her hands shaking. "Excuse me," she said. "I'm collecting signatures for Save the Whales. Will you help us out?"

The man laughed. "Not today," he said in a gravelly voice. He kept walking.

Flossie relaxed. This wasn't so hard. "Don't you like whales?" she asked.

"That has nothing to do with it."

"Then why won't you sign?"

The man stopped and turned around.

Flossie smiled and held the paper out to him. "Pretty please?"

The man snatched it. "Where do I sign?"

"Top line," replied Flossie. She shot a smug glance back to Nan and Freddie.

"All right." The man took the pencil in his left hand and scribbled away.

"Thanks, mister," said Flossie. She stared at the signature. "I can't read it."

"It's Harris," snapped the man. "Simon P. Harris."

Flossie ran back to the others. She showed them the signature.

"Good work," said Nan. "Just what we suspected. The gravelly voice *does* belong to Simon P. Harris. So he's the owner of the Sunset Grill and Jungle Park, too."

Flossie stretched herself up tall. "It was easy," she said.

Nan, Freddie, and Flossie rode their bikes into their driveway.

"Bert's home," said Flossie. "I can hear him practicing his drums in the basement."

They raced downstairs. "Where have you been?" asked Nan.

"Following Danny Rugg," said Bert.

"Anything happen?" Nan wanted to know.

"Nothing," answered Bert. "I shadowed him all day. He squirted Mrs. Bolen's cat with a water gun, and then he practiced his guitar." Bert thumped his bass drum. "Maybe I made a mistake, thinking it was Danny. What did you guys find out?"

Nan filled Bert in, then said, "I think we have two new suspects. Beverly Baku was very angry at Mr. Loomis. She may be making trouble for the park because of her animals."

"And what about that creepy Mr. Eyepatch?" said Flossie.

"Maybe Mr. Harris and Mr. Eyepatch were meeting secretly," Freddie suggested. "I think they're up to something. It looked like they were snooping around."

"Maybe *we* should do a little snooping," said Nan, "after the park closes."

Bert looked at Nan. "Are you sure?"

"There's a fence near the back of the outdoor stage," Nan said. "We can climb it."

"Can we come?" asked Freddie.

"Please?" said Flossie.

Nan shook her head. "Too dangerous."

Freddie flopped down on the couch. "No fair," he said. "I was the one who found the swizzle stick."

What about me?" said Flossie. "I got Simon Harris to sign the paper."

Bert looked at Freddie and Flossie. "Look. If anything happened to you two, Mom and Dad would kill us."

Flossie made a face. She hated being the youngest.

Nan turned to Bert. "The park closes early tonight—at eight," she said. "Are you coming?"

"Might as well," said Bert. "It beats following Danny around."

* * *

At exactly eight-fifteen, Nan and Bert pedaled up behind Jungle Park. They hid their bikes in the bushes behind the fence. "Follow me," Nan whispered. A few minutes later she and Bert had climbed the fence.

The deserted park looked spooky. "Where should we go?" asked Bert.

"To the lions' den," said Nan. She and Bert tiptoed past the outdoor stage. They crept through the shadows of the roller coaster. They walked by Mr. Loomis's trailer. No lights were on inside.

Nan led Bert to the refreshment patio. They stood by the table where she, Flossie, and Freddie had sat that afternoon. "That's where Freddie spotted Mr. Harris," she said, pointing to the counter.

"I don't know what good this is doing," Bert grumbled.

Nan looked up. "Shh. I hear something." She and Bert crouched under a table. A shadow moved past them. The shadow's arms seemed to be signaling to someone.

"I don't like this," Bert whispered. "No one is supposed to be here, right? The park is closed."

"Maybe it's the night watchman," Nan answered.

At that moment, a loud bellow tore through

the night air. It was followed by the sound of glass breaking.

"What was that?" whispered Nan. The ground began to shake. She peeked out and gasped.

An elephant charged past. Its trunk flicked out and picked up a table. It sent the table spinning through the air like a Frisbee.

The elephant grabbed another table and hurled it to the ground. Then it turned.

"Look out!" Nan cried. "It's heading straight for us!"

5
Plan A

"Let's get out of here!" Nan shouted. She and Bert dashed from under the table just as the elephant picked it up and threw it across the patio. It was smashed flat. The elephant trumpeted and stomped its feet.

"C'mon." Bert grabbed Nan's hand.

They dodged an overturned umbrella and leapfrogged a fallen chair. "Bert, look!" cried Nan. "Another one."

A second elephant charged past. Nan and Bert skidded to a stop.

The elephant lowered its trunk and picked up a trash barrel.

"Oh, great," said Nan. "Now he's going to throw it at us."

"Ah-e-ah-e-ah!" Bert beat his chest like Tarzan. The elephant froze. Nan stared.

"Look, it worked in the movies. Ah-e-ah-e-ah," Bert said again. The elephant stood quietly, still holding the barrel.

"Quick," said Bert. "Follow me. And we'd better keep quiet. We don't want anyone to know we're here." They sprinted around the elephant and headed back toward the fence.

Bert reached it first and jumped, grabbing hold of the top. He pulled himself up. "Give me your hand, Nan," he said.

The elephant lumbered toward them, the trash barrel still in its trunk. "Hurry," he said. "That elephant looks mad."

Nan reached up. With one strong tug, Bert pulled her beside him. They jumped to safety as the barrel smashed into the fence.

"Wow!" said Bert. "Are you okay?" Nan nodded numbly. She and Bert were too stunned to move. A siren wailed in the distance.

"The police," said Bert. "Let's get out of here. They'll take care of this." He pulled his bike out from the bushes.

Nan stayed where she was. "Maybe we should tell them . . ." she began.

"Tell them what?" said Bert. "That we saw a shadow? Whoever made it is gone by now. Besides, do you want Mom and Dad to know we came out here tonight?"

"No," said Nan, getting her bike. She could hear the elephants still tossing tables and chairs.

As they pedaled home, Nan said, "We're lucky we weren't squashed."

Bert gripped his handlebars and pedaled faster. Tracking Danny Rugg was one thing. This was different. Whoever was behind this latest stunt wasn't kidding.

The next morning, Bert was awakened by knocking. "Come in," he said. Nan, Flossie, and Freddie flew into his room.

"Listen to this," said Nan. She waved a copy of the *Lakeport News* in his face. " 'Rampaging elephants caused thousands of dollars worth of damage last night at Jungle Park.' "

Bert sat up.

Nan flopped on the bed and read on. " 'This is the worst of several strange events at the park. "It almost looks like someone let those elephants loose on purpose," said park owner Elrod Loomis.' "

Bert jumped out of bed. "That explains the shadow," he said. "Anything else?"

" 'Right now the police have no suspects and no motive,' " Nan read.

"Why would anybody pick on an amusement park?" Freddie wanted to know.

"Beverly Baku hates the old cages at Jungle Park," said Nan. "And her animals are the ones who wrecked the place."

"Let's not forget Mr. Eyepatch," said Flossie.

"Why would he want the park to close down?" asked Bert.

"Maybe he doesn't like rides or animals," suggested Freddie.

"Or ice cream," Flossie added. "What a grouch!"

"Well, someone is doing a great job of scaring people away." Nan shook her head. "No one would want to go to a park where the elephants wreck everything."

"We would!" Bert grabbed his clothes. "We have a rehearsal there this afternoon. It's a perfect excuse to look around."

Nan grinned. "I was just about to say the same thing," she said.

"Can we come?" asked Freddie.

"Yeah," said Flossie. "We *always* have to stay home."

Bert looked at Nan. "Okay," he said. "But try not to act too weird. We don't want anyone to get suspicious."

That afternoon the Bobbseys squeezed into the family station wagon. Bert sat between Freddie and Flossie. He glanced anxiously at his drum set in the back.

Hidden inside the bass drum was Freddie's fingerprinting kit. Bert was carrying his Rex Sleuther Pocket Crime-Solver. It was a folding pocketknife with all sorts of gadgets on it.

"When will your rehearsal be over?" asked Mrs. Bobbsey. She stopped the car at the entrance to Jungle Park.

Bert looked at the others. "Could you pick us up at four-thirty?" he asked.

"Okay," his mother replied. The twins piled out of the car.

The Aliens practiced long and hard that afternoon. Bert had never been to a better rehearsal.

"It just shows what we can do when people aren't trying to mess us up," Bert said.

As soon as Brian and Jimmy had gone, Freddie rushed up to Bert. "Can we go spy now?" he asked.

"Shh," Bert hissed. "Not so loud! Let's go over to the elephant cages."

The Bobbseys ran across the park. They found a crowd looking at the elephants.

"Now what?" whispered Nan. "We can't dust the lock for fingerprints with all these people here."

Bert smiled. "Plan A," he said. He took Flossie by the hand and led her around the corner. "You know what to do."

Flossie nodded.

Bert left Flossie and hurried back to Nan. "Almost ready," he said, grinning.

A scream filled the air. "Mommy," cried Flossie. "Where's my mommy? I lost her!"

The crowd at the elephant cages rushed around the corner.

Nan smiled. "Works every time."

Bert bent over the lock. "Hand me the fingerprint—" He banged on the gate.

"We're too late. The cops have already dusted for fingerprints. See the powder? And there aren't any prints!" He pulled out his Pocket Crime-Solver. "We need the magnifying glass."

"What for?" asked Freddie.

"Checking for footprints," Bert answered.

Freddie helped him circle the cement around the cages. "No luck here," he said.

"Let's look where we saw the shadow," said Nan.

"Good idea," agreed Bert. He could hear Flossie still wailing in the background.

"Uh-oh," said Nan. "We forgot about Flossie. I'll go get her and meet you guys by the tables."

"Okay," said Bert. "C'mon, Freddie."

Freddie and Bert searched the patio.

"Any luck?" asked Nan when she returned. Flossie was eating a triple-dip strawberry ice cream cone.

"Nope," said Bert. "Too many people have been here."

Flossie slurped her ice cream.

"Where did you get that?" asked Freddie.

"A waitress gave it to me when I was crying," she said.

Freddie scowled. "No fair."

Flossie took another bite. "You think it's easy to cry like that?" she asked.

"Maybe we should check on Beverly Baku," Nan said suddenly.

"Yeah!" cried Freddie. "She warned us that something like this might happen."

Nan nodded. "And she knows how to handle elephants. I wonder where she was when they got loose."

"That's it!" said Flossie. "We solved the whole thing."

Bert held up his hand. "Slow down, Flossie," he said. "Why would Beverly want to put the park out of business?"

Flossie shrugged her shoulders. "I don't know."

"We should still talk to her," said Freddie.

"Yeah!" said Flossie. "And I can pretend I'm doing a report on elephants."

The twins searched Jungle Kingdom but couldn't find Beverly Baku.

"Where else should we look?" asked Freddie.

Nan smiled. "I know someone who can tell us where she is."

Several minutes later, Bert knocked on the door to Mr. Loomis's trailer. "Come in," called a voice. Bert opened the door. Mr. Loomis was eating a pastrami sandwich and reading the sports page of the newspaper.

"Remember us?" asked Nan, following Bert and Freddie into the trailer.

Mr. Loomis nodded. "What can I do for you?"

"Have you seen Beverly Baku?" asked Nan. "My sister is doing a report on elephants."

Mr. Loomis gobbled down the last of his sandwich. "She's gone," he said, wiping his lips with a paper towel. "Left for a vacation in Kenya."

Mr. Loomis began to laugh. " 'Tiny,' she said. . . ." He looked up. "That's what everyone calls me, *Tiny*. Silly name for a big guy like me." He patted his belly.

" 'Tiny,' she said, 'you ought to come to Africa with me. And bring all the animals with you. Set them free.' "

Tiny shook his head. "Maybe I should have set them free. Then the elephants wouldn't have caused all this trouble."

"When did Beverly leave?" asked Nan.

"Yesterday afternoon," Tiny replied. "I drove her to the airport myself."

Bert nodded. That means she couldn't have been around last night, he thought. "Well, I guess it's time to go," he said loudly. "Too bad,

Flossie. You'll have to find someone else to help with your report."

He reached for the doorknob, but the door was already opening.

A tall man entered, carrying a big wrench. At first, all Bert saw was a mass of red hair.

Then the man looked up. It was Mr. Eye-patch!

6

Hold On!

Flossie's knees shook. But Mr. Eyepatch just walked in.

"Have you finished working on the roller coaster?" Tiny asked.

The man grinned and patted the wrench with his left hand.

Flossie couldn't take her eyes away from that black eyepatch. Even when he smiled, Mr. Eyepatch looked mean.

"Good work," said Tiny. "You can go home. I'll run the roller coaster to make sure it works okay. Tomorrow you can start on the merry-go-round."

Mr. Eyepatch nodded and left the trailer.

"Hey, I've got an idea," said Tiny. "How would you kids like to ride on our new, improved roller coaster?"

"Great!" said Freddie.

Tiny clapped his hands. "Everyone out," he said. "This is going to be fun."

Flossie put her hand on her forehead. "I don't feel so good," she said.

Nan grabbed Flossie's arm. "Oh, no, you don't," she said. "Every time we want to ride on the roller coaster, you say no. Then when we get you on, you stay for seven rides." She shoved Flossie toward the door.

"Okay, okay," Flossie grumbled. She followed Nan out.

Tiny led the Bobbseys to the first car of the roller coaster. In each car was a long, wide seat with a safety bar across it. "Who's the bravest?" he said.

"Flossie," said Freddie. "She loves roller coasters."

Flossie glared at Freddie, but it was too late. Tiny had picked her up. "You get to ride in the front car, then," he said. He put Freddie next to her.

Tiny pointed at Bert and Nan. "You climb into the second car."

When they were ready, the cars began to move. The roller coaster chugged slowly up the first hill. This was the part Flossie hated. She didn't mind zooming down. It was the *waiting* that drove her crazy.

Flossie looked over the side at the ground

below. Mr. Eyepatch was heading for the fun house. He stopped to look up at the roller coaster. Then he saw Flossie peering down at him. He began to wave both his arms.

That's funny, Flossie thought. He didn't seem so friendly before. She waved back, but Mr. Eyepatch had stopped waving. He was running for the fun house. What a weird guy! thought Flossie.

With a jolt, the car stopped. It had reached the top of the first hill. Flossie gripped the safety bar.

"Here we go," yelled Freddie.

Flossie closed her eyes and felt the roller coaster start down the hill and pick up speed. There was no other feeling like it in the world. "Wheeeeeeee!" she screamed, bouncing in her seat.

The car rounded a sharp curve. A jolt made Flossie lose her grip on the safety bar.

"Hold on!" Bert yelled.

Flossie grabbed the bar just as a second jolt rocked the car.

"Something's wrong," Freddie shouted.

Flossie peered over her shoulder at the cable between their car and Nan and Bert's. *Ping-ping*. The wire strands were breaking.

Twang. The cable snapped apart!

"Flossie!" yelled Nan. She leaned forward and grabbed the back of the first car.

Flossie was white as a ghost. She hung over the side, waving her arms. "HELLLLLLPPPP!" she screamed.

Bert grabbed the first car, too. "Flossie! Freddie! Hang on!" he shouted.

Flossie and Freddie turned to grab the second car. The roller coaster whipped around another corner. The cars rocked dangerously. "Stop the ride!" shouted Freddie.

Flossie's arms ached. She couldn't hold on for long. She searched the ground for Tiny. Why wasn't he watching?

The roller coaster started down another steep hill. Flossie spotted Tiny leaving the trailer. "Tiny!" she screamed. "Help!"

Tiny glanced up and waved.

"Stop the ride," Bert yelled. "It's broken!"

Tiny looked puzzled.

"IT'S BROKEN!" shouted Freddie, at the top of his lungs.

Tiny stared at the roller coaster. A look of understanding crossed his face. He ran for the controls. Within seconds, the cars had come to a halt near Tiny.

Nan had been holding on so tight that she had to pry her fingers loose from the car. She used the safety bar to steady herself and slowly stood up.

"What happened?" asked Tiny.

"The cable broke," Nan replied. "It just pulled apart in the middle of the ride."

Tiny was angry. "This was all supposed to be fixed," he said. He picked up one end of the broken cable.

Nan gasped and nudged Bert.

Bert gave a low whistle. "That cable was deliberately cut. Destroyed."

Tiny's voice was grim. "Where is that repairman?"

"I knew it!" said Flossie. "He *is* a bad guy!" Then she remembered what she'd seen from the roller coaster. "He was headed for the fun house! I just saw him!"

"Lots of places to hide in there," said Tiny. "Do you kids want to help me search?"

"You bet!" said the Bobbseys.

They followed Tiny to the fun house. He stopped at the entrance to talk to the ticket taker. "No more customers till I give the word," he said.

The fun house was dark inside. Eerie laughter echoed as the Bobbseys walked forward. This isn't going to be easy, thought Flossie.

She could see openings into dark tunnels. The walls around them had been painted to look like giant mouths.

"Bert, you and Freddie take the green tunnel," Nan called. "Flossie and I will take the red one. Tiny, you take the blue tunnel."

"Right," said Tiny. "Let's go."

Whoosh! Flossie and Nan found themselves on a chute. They flew through darkness, to land on a big pillow. Moving forward, they walked through shadows. Once they wound up in a brightly lit maze of mirrors. But they found no trace of Mr. Eyepatch.

"Maybe you were wrong," Nan said. "I bet he never even came in here. He just— aaaaaaaaaaaaaah!"

A figure leaped at them from the darkness. Nan and Flossie jumped back. It was just a dummy.

"I hate fun houses," said Nan. She walked up to the dummy. "Hey, what's this?"

Flossie saw Nan pull a handful of red hair from behind the dummy's foot.

Nan shook it out. It was a wig. Two things fell to the floor—a fake mustache and a black eyepatch.

"We'll never find Mr. Eyepatch now," said Nan. "He was wearing a disguise!"

7

The Problem Is . . .

Nan called the other searchers and showed them the wig, mustache, and eyepatch. Tiny agreed to hold on to them for Lieutenant Pike. Freddie and Flossie helped Nan and Bert collect their equipment from the stage. Then the Bobbseys went to the park entrance to wait for their mother.

"Have a good time, kids?" asked Mrs. Bobbsey after the kids and equipment were settled in the car.

"It was, um, interesting," replied Bert. Nobody else said anything until they were home. Then Nan, Bert, Freddie, and Flossie sat under a tree in the backyard. They tried to clear up the case.

"So, what have we got?" asked Bert. "We started out with two suspects, Beverly Baku and Mr. Eyepatch. Beverly is in Africa—"

"And Mr. Eyepatch turned out to be a phony," said Nan. "Just a wig, a mustache, and a black patch. He could be anybody."

"What about Danny Rugg?" asked Freddie.

Bert shook his head. "Danny might have set the smoke bomb, but I can't see him cutting the roller coaster cable. We could have been killed!"

"I don't know about that," said Nan. "The roller coaster was going to run empty."

"Is that why Mr. Eyepatch was waving?" wondered Flossie. "Did he try to warn us?"

Freddie frowned. "No one knew we were going on the roller coaster except Tiny."

Flossie clenched her fist. "Yeah! And he *wanted* us to ride it."

"That makes no sense," said Bert. "Why would Tiny try to close down his own park?"

"And what about Mr. Eyepatch?" asked Nan. "He must have been the one who cut the cable."

"Well, *he's* not Tiny," said Bert. He scratched his head. "The problem is . . ."

"The problem is TINY!" Freddie burst out. "That's what I heard Simon Harris say at the Sunset Grill."

"When was this?" asked Nan.

"Before you followed me back there." Freddie frowned, remembering. "He was on the telephone, and he said, 'The problem is *tiny*.' I thought it was funny. Why was he getting upset over a tiny problem?"

"He wasn't talking about the *size* of his problem," Nan said. "He was talking *about* his problem—Tiny Loomis!"

"Simon Harris and Tiny are partners in Jungle Park," said Bert. "Maybe Tiny is working with Mr. Eyepatch to make trouble at the park?" Bert paused. "Maybe they're trying to force the park out of business."

"Why?" asked Flossie.

"I don't know," said Nan. "But don't worry. Jungle Park won't close if *we* have anything to say about it."

Nan brushed her hair out of her eyes. It was the next afternoon, and the Bobbseys were biking their way to the park. Nan looked ahead. Bert was about ten feet in front of her. "You can't catch me!" he sang.

Nan pedaled faster. Bert always beat her on his bike. She turned around to check on Freddie and Flossie, far behind.

Freddie was waving. Nan waved back. Freddie shouted and waved again.

"I can't hear you," Nan yelled.

Just then, a red van zoomed up, almost running Nan off the road.

"Hey, watch it!" she shouted. Then she stared. No wonder Freddie was trying to get her attention. Simon Harris was driving!

Nan stuck her fingers in her mouth and whistled. Bert slowed down just as the van passed him. "What's up?" he yelled.

"That's Mr. Harris's van," called Nan.

"Really!" Bert bent down and sped off.

The van pulled through the back gate of the park, with Bert right behind. Nan and the others raced up. When they reached the gate, neither Bert nor the van was in sight.

"They must have gone around this corner," Nan said. "Otherwise, we'd see them." She turned the corner. Flossie and Freddie followed. They rode past some sheds and garages. Then the road became deserted.

"I hope Bert's okay," said Flossie.

"Me, too," said Nan. "We didn't go this way the other night." They passed a grove of fruit trees. At the end of a long dirt road, Nan spotted the parked van.

Bert popped up from behind some bushes. He put his finger to his lips. "Quiet," he said. "We don't want anyone to see us."

"Why did Mr. Harris stop out here in the middle of nowhere?" asked Flossie.

"I think he's waiting for someone," Bert

whispered. "Maybe he doesn't want Tiny to know about it. Leave the bikes here. Maybe we can sneak up closer."

Nan, Flossie, and Freddie nodded and climbed off their bikes. Then Nan stopped. "What was that?" she asked.

A huge yellow truck came roaring up.

"Hide!" shouted Bert.

The four children dropped to the ground. "Look! There's a tunnel under the road!" said Freddie. The kids squeezed into an empty drainage tunnel.

The truck screeched to a halt a little way down the road. Everything was quiet. "I'm going to have a look," Bert whispered.

Nan grabbed his arm. "Are you crazy?"

"I'll be careful," said Bert. He wormed his way out of the drainage tunnel. Then he snapped back in. "That truck is parked right next to the red van."

Nan, Flossie, and Freddie squeezed closer. "Let me see," said Freddie.

Bert grabbed his collar. "Stay where you are, pal," he said. "This is no time for sight-seeing." Bert carefully eased himself a few inches out of the tunnel again.

"The driver of the truck is getting out now," he whispered. "As soon as he's far enough away, we should be able to come out."

"Can you see the truck?" said Nan. "I

thought I saw something painted on the side."

"You're right," he said. "Peabody Construction Company."

"Peabody Construction," Nan repeated. "That sounds familiar." She shook her head. "I don't know why, but I think it's the answer to this mystery!"

8

Trouble on the Way

"I wouldn't worry about that," Bert whispered. "How do we get out of here?"

"What's happening, Bert?" asked Nan.

"Freddie is squishing me in here," complained Flossie.

"Shh," said Nan. "Stop wiggling."

"Mr. Harris got out of his van," Bert reported. "He's walking over to the man in the yellow truck. They're shaking hands. Now they're busy talking. Let's move."

One by one, the Bobbseys squirmed from the tunnel. "Be quiet," Bert whispered. "I want to hear what those two are saying."

Bert crawled forward. It was no use. Mr. Harris and the other man were talking too

softly. Bert wished he had a Rex Sleuther Long-Distance Earphone. The ad said you could listen to a conversation from as far away as fifty feet. He sighed as the two men shook hands. Then they headed back to their trucks. "Heads down!" Bert whispered.

"We'll talk again soon," Mr. Harris called from his van. "I want to see those plans you've drawn up."

"Good," said the other man.

"What plans?" said Nan. Bert shrugged.

The yellow truck drove back the way it had come. Simon Harris's red van headed deeper into Jungle Park.

"Give them a minute or two," said Nan. "We want to make sure they're out of the way. Then we'll get our bikes." Her face was thoughtful. "I wonder if Dad could tell us anything about Peabody Construction."

As soon as the Bobbseys got home, they ran to the kitchen. Mr. Bobbsey was at the counter, stirring a sauce.

"Mmmm," said Flossie, taking a deep sniff. "Are you making barbecues?"

Mr. Bobbsey laughed. "I thought I'd grill some chicken tonight. Sound good?"

"Yes," chorused the children.

Nan cleared her throat. "Dad," she began,

"do you know a company named Peabody Construction?"

Mr. Bobbsey tasted the sauce. "Delicious," he said. "Peabody?" he repeated.

"They drive big yellow trucks," said Freddie.

Mr. Bobbsey nodded. "Peabody Construction specializes in building shopping malls. One of their men came in to see me about building supplies." Mr. Bobbsey owned a lumberyard.

"So they're going to build a mall around here?" Nan asked.

"Well, they've been looking," said Mr. Bobbsey. "I guess they're finally making a deal."

Bert's heart raced. "Did he say that?"

"He just mentioned some big landlord in town." Mr. Bobbsey added a little onion powder to the sauce.

"Simon Harris?" asked Nan.

Mr. Bobbsey looked up. "That's the name," he said. "Now that I've answered your questions, will you answer one for me? What's going on?"

Nan grinned. "You just helped us clear up the Jungle Park mystery."

"I did?" said Mr. Bobbsey.

"He did?" said Bert.

"Well, it all makes sense, now," Nan went on. "We know that Jungle Park hasn't been making money. Tiny Loomis told us that. I'll bet Mr. Harris *wants* the park to shut down. Then he can sell it to Peabody Construction so they can build a shopping mall. He'd make a lot of money that way."

"What about Tiny Loomis?" asked Bert.

"Mr. Harris and Tiny are partners," said Nan. "They have to agree on shutting down Jungle Park. And Tiny doesn't want to."

Nan smiled at Freddie. "Freddie heard Mr. Harris say it himself—'The problem is Tiny.' "

Bert nodded. "Tiny won't close the place. So you think Mr. Harris made those accidents happen."

"We *saw* him setting up accidents," Nan said. "He was the shadow at the elephants' cages. He also worked on the roller coaster. We just didn't recognize him. Look here."

She picked up a piece of paper and drew quickly. She held up a sketch of a bald, frowning man. "Who is this?"

"Simon Harris," Freddie answered. "It looks just like him."

"Okay." Nan began adding to her sketch. "Draw curly hair and a bushy mustache. Who have we got?" She held up the picture.

"Mr. Eyepatch!" Freddie shouted.

Nan drew in the eyepatch. "That's why he never spoke to anybody. Simon Harris could hide his face but not his voice."

"There was another thing he couldn't hide," Nan went on. "Flossie, do you remember when Mr. Harris signed your petition? He used his left hand. And when Mr. Eyepatch showed us where the stage was, he pointed with—"

"His left hand!" Flossie broke in.

"That's right!" said Nan.

"Tiny Loomis mentioned that Harris was paying Mr. Eyepatch out of his own pocket," added Bert.

"And as the repairman, he could go all over the park," said Nan. "That left him free to set up all the accidents."

"The smoke bomb on the stage," said Bert, "and the elephants, and the roller coaster."

"That makes a lot of sense," said Mr. Bobbsey. "I think you should call Lieutenant Pike."

The twins crowded around the phone. "Let me do the talking," said Bert. He picked up the receiver and dialed.

Lieutenant Pike was quiet as Bert explained what they'd found out. Then he said, "You'd better stay where you are. I'll send some of my people to the park. And I'll take you over there myself—say, in an hour."

"Great," said Bert. He hung up. "He'll be here after dinner," he told the others.

"But we've got our final performance tonight," Nan reminded him. "We have to take our equipment."

"Your mother and I will bring it," said Mr. Bobbsey. "We'll meet you there."

An hour later, the Bobbseys were in the back of Lieutenant Pike's patrol car. "Your call was very helpful," the lieutenant said. "We've suspected the repairman for some time now." He shook his head. "But we hadn't made the connection with Simon Harris."

A muffled report came in over the police radio. Lieutenant Pike listened closely and then picked up his microphone. "This is Car Eighty-five," he said. "We're on our way."

He turned to the backseat. "My people are at the park now," he said. "And they're all on the lookout for Simon Harris."

"Can you turn on the siren?" asked Flossie.

"This isn't a toy, Flossie," Nan said.

Flossie stuck out her bottom lip.

Lieutenant Pike looked in the rearview mirror and smiled. "I was just about to." He reached over and flipped on the siren.

"Yay!" said Flossie. "Step on it!"

Two minutes later, the car pulled up at Jungle Park. Another police car was guarding the front gates.

"Any luck?" Lieutenant Pike asked the officer on duty.

"Haven't found him yet, sir," said the policeman. "But we know what he looks like."

71

"What if he wears another disguise?" Freddie asked.

"We know what to expect now," said Lieutenant Pike. He led them to the park office.

Sitting behind his desk, Tiny looked sad. "My own partner was trying to ruin the park," he said. "It's hard to believe."

"Do you have any idea where he might be?" asked Lieutenant Pike.

Tiny shrugged. "Last time I saw him, he was headed for the stage."

Bert glanced at his watch and felt sick to his stomach. The stage! The Aliens were scheduled to play there in thirty minutes!

9

Monkey Business

"I'm sure Mr. Harris is rigging up another accident," said Nan. "We've got to get to the stage."

"You're right." Lieutenant Pike spoke into a radio. A squad car pulled up, and Lieutenant Pike and the twins climbed in.

The police car drove carefully through the park. "We don't want to worry anyone," Nan whispered to her brothers and sister. "Just act natural while we search. Bert, you and Flossie check the far side of the stage. Freddie and I will take the other side. If you see Mr. Harris, get the police."

She frowned. "And I guess we should look out for anything that's been left where it shouldn't be."

The police car stopped. "I want you kids to stay out of the way," said Lieutenant Pike.

Nan smiled. "Okay," she said sweetly.

The Bobbseys waited until the police got busy.

"Now," whispered Nan. Bert and Flossie nodded. They strolled casually to the other side of the stage. Nan and Freddie began to inspect every inch of their side.

"Ahoy!" shouted Danny Rugg. He was already in his costume. Time was running out.

"This is the big night," said Danny. He drew his sword and lunged at the curtain.

"Right," said Nan. Great, she thought. I have to waste time talking to Danny.

Danny narrowed his eyes. "You guys don't look too ready," he said.

"It just takes a minute to change," Nan told him. "Besides, you're on first."

"Why are all these cops here?" Danny asked.

"Uh, security," she replied.

Danny raised his eyebrows.

"Didn't you hear?" said Nan. "Paul Van Martin of the Airheads is going to be one of the judges tonight."

Danny's jaw dropped. "*The* Paul Van Martin?" he asked.

Nan nodded. "His limo is arriving at the front gate in fifteen minutes."

Danny shoved his sword back into its sheath.

"Wow!" he said. "Wait till I tell the guys." He dashed off.

"Is that true?" Freddie asked.

Nan grinned. "Of course not. I said it so he'd leave us alone. Let's get to work."

Nan and Freddie kept looking, but it was hopeless. She signaled to Bert.

"What's up?" he asked, crossing the stage.

The theater had begun to fill up. "No trace of Mr. Harris," said Nan. "Let's go talk to Tiny. Maybe he can help us out."

Tiny was bent over his desk, writing checks.

"Hi," said Nan. "We're back."

"What now?" he asked. "More bad news?"

"Nobody's found Mr. Harris," Bert said. "If there's going to be an accident on that stage"— he shrugged—"we can't find any clues to it."

Tiny shook his head. "I still can't believe Simon Harris would do this to me. Sure, we had some fights about selling the place. But I thought I'd convinced him to keep it. We were even fixing the place up." He sighed. "I guess Simon always was a money guy. He didn't understand about having fun."

"What do you mean?" asked Flossie.

"He just put up the money to build this place," Tiny explained. "It could have been a parking lot, for all he cared. He'd made a lot of money and wanted to invest it in something— anything."

"How did he make his money?" Nan asked.

Tiny shrugged. "Electric signs," he said. "He had a company that put up big electric signs. Like the one up there." He pointed at the huge Jungle Park sign shining over the stage.

Nan and Bert stared at each other. "We checked the stage," they both said, "but we never checked up there!"

Nan grabbed Flossie's hand. "Let's go," she said. "Time is running out."

"Where are we going?" asked Flossie.

"Back to the stage," replied Bert. "Before someone gets hurt."

Nan shoved her way through the crowds. She stopped outside the stage door. "Flossie, you and Freddie wait here," she said.

"Why can't we come inside?" asked Freddie.

"We need you to be on the lookout for Mr. Harris," said Bert.

The stage manager was leaning against the wall chewing on a toothpick. "Has Mr. Harris been here today?" asked Nan.

"Haven't seen him," drawled the stage manager.

Bert hurried to the ladder that led to the sign. The metal rattled as he started up.

"Hey," said the stage manager. "You can't go up there."

Nan grabbed the bottom rung. "We have to," she said. "It's a special effect for our act."

Taking a deep breath, she started up the shaking ladder.

It was a long climb. And a scary one. But finally, they reached the metal walkway at the bottom of the sign.

Bert took a deep breath. "Look at the other end of the sign. Someone is bent over those wires." He and Nan started to creep forward. Then they stopped and stared. "That's a gorilla!" Bert exclaimed.

"So what?" Nan said. "There are people in animal suits all over the park."

"Fixing wires? I think I know who's under that suit." Bert pulled out his Crime-Solver and turned on the built-in flashlight. Shining it across the walkway, he yelled, "Mr. Harris, we know it's you."

The gorilla jumped up. But Bert and Nan were blocking the ladder.

"Come on, Mr. Harris," said Bert. "You might as well give up."

The gorilla ran the other way. He wrapped his arms around a thick pipe and slid out of sight.

Bert ran back to the ladder. "Come on! We can't let him get away!"

Nan gripped the ladder. It was shaking wildly from Bert's descent. "This is going to be a great trip," she moaned.

* * *

Outside the stage door, Flossie was having problems. Freddie was being a pain.

"Let go of my arm," he said. "I'm going whether you like it or not. We never get to do the exciting stuff."

Flossie held tight. "You're going to get into trouble," she told him. "Nan wants us to stay right here."

"If you don't let go, you'll be sorry," said Freddie. He shook his arm.

"All right!" said Flossie. "Go! Get in trouble! See if I care!"

The stage door opened, and a man wearing a gorilla costume stepped out. Flossie didn't pay any attention. Lots of people dressed up in animal costumes at Jungle Park.

Freddie grinned and stepped forward. "Hi, Mr. Gorilla," he said.

The gorilla pushed past him, knocking Freddie over. "Out of my way, kid," he snarled in a familiar gravelly voice.

Freddie sat up and gasped. "It's him!" he shouted. "Get that gorilla!"

10

Get That Gorilla!

The gorilla jumped over Freddie and ran. Freddie was right on his heels. "Come back here," he yelled. Flossie raced ahead.

"I'll get him," she cried.

Freddie sped up. Mr. Harris was having a tough time in his bulky costume.

"Halt! Police!" shouted a voice. Turning, Freddie saw two policemen join the chase.

Mr. Harris ran to the refreshment patio. "Out of my way," he yelled. He pushed past a little girl and knocked over a trash barrel. It looked for a moment as if he might fall.

Freddie and Flossie drew closer.

Mr. Harris darted to the right, looking over his shoulder.

That's why he didn't see the stack of empty cartons in his path. As Mr. Harris crashed into the cartons, Freddie jumped. He grabbed Mr. Harris's leg. "Gotcha!" he cried. Flossie grabbed the other leg.

"Let go of me!" shouted Mr. Harris.

Freddie and Flossie hung on. Mr. Harris fell. Seconds later, the two policemen had him in handcuffs. "Good work, kids," they said.

Freddie looked at Flossie and grinned. "Now *that*," he said breathlessly, "was exciting!"

Bert and Nan came rushing up with more policemen. The police removed the gorilla head. But something fell from the fur suit, clanging on the ground.

"A hacksaw!" shouted Freddie.

Another tool clattered to the ground. "Wire cutters!" exclaimed Bert. "What were you going to do to that sign?"

"All right, you caught me," Simon Harris said. "I was fixing the wires to blow every light in the park. Everything would go dark when the first band began to play."

"Gee," Bert whispered to Nan. "Too bad we didn't let him do that. The Skulls would have been playing then."

"I never meant to hurt anyone," Mr. Harris went on. "Just to scare them away."

"So you could sell the park to Peabody Construction," said Nan.

"What about that roller coaster?" said Bert. "We could have been killed!"

"I didn't know you would be riding in it." Simon Harris shook his head. "I thought Tiny would run it empty the first time. The cars would pull apart, then crash. And that would be the end of the coaster."

He looked up at them. "By the time I saw you on the ride, it was too late. I did try to warn you."

"So *that's* why you were waving at me," said Flossie.

"Well, it's all over now," said Lieutenant Pike. The police led Simon Harris away.

Freddie jumped up and down. "We caught the crook!" he said. "Flossie and I tackled him!"

Nan knelt down and hugged Freddie and Flossie. "You were great," she said.

Lieutenant Pike smiled. "There won't be any more accidents at Jungle Park."

Rock music suddenly filled the park.

"The Skulls!" said Bert. He turned to Lieutenant Pike. "We've got to go—or there *will* be another accident. If we don't get into costume, the Aliens will be late!"

"I'll give you a lift," said Lieutenant Pike. He grinned at Flossie. "We'll even run the siren."

"I hope Bert and Nan are ready," said Freddie. He and Flossie were standing in the wings of the stage. "The Skulls are almost finished."

Danny Rugg gave a loud twang on his guitar and bowed. The contest director came out onstage. "Let's hear it for the Skulls!" he said.

The crowd clapped and cheered. Then the curtains closed. Freddie and Flossie could hear the director outside the curtain. While he gave the rules for the Battle of the Bands, workmen set up the Aliens' equipment.

"What's Danny doing over there?" asked Flossie.

"I can't see. It's pretty dark with the spotlights off." Freddie strained his eyes. "He's sticking something behind a speaker." He turned to his sister. "Uh-oh."

The Aliens had never played better. The audience whistled and cheered.

"Listen to that applause!" The contest director smiled. "I think we have a winner in our Battle of the Bands!"

The crowd cheered louder.

"And now, to present the prize, here's the owner of Jungle Park."

Tiny Loomis walked onto the stage. "I'm pleased to present the first prize," he said. "A brand-new set of microphones." He handed the prize to Nan and Bert.

Brian and Jimmy were grinning and clapping. "Congratulations to the Aliens," Tiny said.

Nan smiled and waved at the audience. All their practice and hard work had paid off.

Bert whispered something in Tiny's ear.

"Isn't that nice," Tiny said. "The Aliens think the Skulls should get a special hand. Danny Rugg, come on up."

Danny stumbled onstage. It looked as if he'd been pushed on.

"Over here, Danny," Bert said. "Right by this speaker."

"Oh, that's all right." Danny smiled nervously.

Bert put his arm around Danny. He pulled him over to the speaker, away from the microphones. "Smile for the folks, Danny."

"Let me out of here!" Danny said. He couldn't take his eyes off the speaker.

"What are you looking at?" Nan whispered. "You'd think that speaker was going to explode."

"Um . . . uh," said Danny.

Bert reached behind the speaker. He pulled out a little package. "Here's your stink bomb," he whispered. "We knew you put it there. But we wanted to beat you fair and square." He looked out at the cheering crowd. "And we did! Don't worry. We fixed the bomb. It won't go off now."

The crowd kept cheering. "You'd have been in trouble if it had gone off," Bert went on. "They just caught the guy who was causing all the accidents here."

Danny kept a sick smile on his face as he looked out at the audience. "Well," he whispered, "at least I'll get to meet Paul Van Martin."

"Um, no," said Nan. "I just told you that to get you out of the way. The police were closing in to catch the guy. Paul Van Martin isn't really here."

The audience finally stopped cheering. Tiny Loomis smiled and waved. "Thank you all for coming," he said. The curtain closed.

Danny Rugg slunk off. "They even lied to me about Paul Van Martin," he grumbled.

Bert slapped Nan on the back. "We did it!" he hooted. "Yippee!"

Nan grinned at her brother and then ran her fingers through her silver hair. "I don't know about you, but I'd love to get out of this junk."

"Nah!" said Bert. "Let's go on some of the rides."

Freddie, Flossie, and Mr. and Mrs. Bobbsey came up. "Congratulations!" they all said at once.

Flossie tugged on Nan's skirt. "Tiny said we can go on as many rides as we want tonight," she said. "For free!"

Nan threw up her arms. "Okay, okay! I guess no one will mind a couple of Aliens taking over. Anyway, it sure beats gorillas."

Bert leaned down to pick up the microphones and laughed. "Don't worry, Nan," he said. "Now that Mr. Harris is gone, we can be sure of one thing."

"What's that?" said Nan.

Bert gave a sly grin. "From now on," he said, "there'll be no more monkey business!"

___**THE DASTARDLY MURDER OF DIRTY PETE**
Eth Clifford   55835/$2.50

___**THE VAMPIRE MOVES IN**
Angela Sommer-Bodenburg   55422/$2.50

___**ME, MY GOAT, AND MY SISTER'S WEDDING**
Stella Pevsner   62422/$2.50

___**JUDGE BENJAMIN: THE SUPERDOG RESCUE**
Judith Whitelock McInerney   54202/$2.50

___**DANGER ON PANTHER PEAK**
Bill Marshall   61282/$2.50

___**THIRD PRIZE SURPRISE: BAD NEWS BUNNY #1**
Susan Saunders   62713/$2.50

___**BACK TO NATURE: BAD NEWS BUNNY #2**
Susan Saunders   62714/$2.50

___**STOP THE PRESSES!: BAD NEWS BUNNY #3**
Susan Saunders   62715/$2.50

___**WHO'S GOT A SECRET?: BAD NEWS BUNNY #4**
Susan Saunders   62716/$2.50

___**ME AND THE TERRIBLE TWO**
Ellen Conford   63666/$2.50

___**THE CASE OF THE HORRIBLE SWAMP MONSTER**
Drew Stevenson   62693/$2.50

___**WHO NEEDS A BRATTY BROTHER?**
Linda Gondosh   62777/$2.50